BOYZ RULE!

Race Car Dreamers

Felice Arena and Phil Kettle

illustrated by
Bettina Guthridge

P9-BJF-228

First published 2003 by
MACMILLAN EDUCATION AUSTRALIA PTY LTD
627 Chapel Street, South Yarra, Australia 3141

Copyright © Felice Arena and Phil Kettle 2003

This edition first published in the United States of America
in 2004 by MONDO Publishing.

All rights reserved.
No part of this publication may be reproduced, except in the case of
quotation for articles or reviews, or stored in any retrieval system, or
transmitted in any form or by any means, electronic, mechanical,
photocopying, recording, or otherwise, without written permission
from the publisher.

For information contact:
MONDO Publishing
980 Avenue of the Americas
New York, NY 10018

Visit our web site at http://www.mondopub.com

04 05 06 07 08 09   9 8 7 6 5 4 3 2 1

ISBN 1-59336-375-3 (PB)

Library of Congress Cataloging-in-Publication Data

Arena, Felice, 1968-
   Race car dreamers / Felice Arena and Phil Kettle ; illustrated by
   Bettina Guthridge.
   p. cm. -- (Boyz rule!)
   ISBN: 1-59336-375-3 (pbk.)
   [1. Dreaming of being race car drivers, Josh and Con decide to build a
   racing kart. Includes simple karting facts and questions to test the reader's
   comprehension. 2. Karting--Fiction. 3. Automobile racing--Fiction.] I. Kettle,
   Phil, 1955- II. Guthridge, Bettina, ill. III. Title.

PZ7.A6825Rac 2004
[E]--dc22
                                                          2004040281

Project Management by Limelight Press Pty Ltd
Cover and text design by Lore Foye
Illustrations by Bettina Guthridge

Printed in Hong Kong

Contents

Josh   Con

CHAPTER 1

The Idea

Josh and Con are sitting in an old car in Con's garage. The car is on a set of blocks—it has no wheels. The best friends talk about what it would be like to be race car drivers.

Con "Imagine if we were old enough
to race. How cool would that be?"

Josh "Yeah, it'd be unreal. Look
out, Jeff Gordan, here we come!"

Con "I wish it was ten years from
now and then we could race this
car."

Josh "Yeah, but it'd be kinda hard
in a car that doesn't move."

Con "Maybe we could build our own race car?"

Josh "What? Now? Cool."

Con "I bet there's enough stuff here in the garage to build the best race car in the world."

Josh "What are we going to use for an engine?"

Con "Maybe we could make a car without an engine and just race it down some hill."

Josh "Yeah, but then it won't be a car exactly."

Con "I know, but it'll be the next best thing."

Josh "What?"

Con "A go-kart!"

CHAPTER 2

Wheels and More

Con and Josh hunt through the garage to find things that they can use to build their go-kart. They pile it all up in the middle of the garage floor.

Con "Okay, I think we've got everything we need."

Josh "The only thing that we don't have is... "

Con "Is what?"

Josh "We don't have any wheels."

Con "Yeah, I know, we've gotta get some."

Josh "From where?"

Con thinks for a moment—his hands on his hips and his face all screwed up.

Josh "I know where!"

Con "Where?"

Josh "From my sister's bike. She hardly ever uses it."

Con "Cool! But that's only two wheels. We still need to find another two."

The boys stand still and start to think again.

Con "Maybe...I could take the wheels off my father's golf cart?"

Josh "Great idea! We'll put them back after we've finished racing the kart."

Con "And we can put the wheels back on your sister's bike, too."

Josh "It's a plan! I'll go and get my sister's bike wheels and you get the wheels from your father's golf cart."

CHAPTER 3

Go-Kart Builders

Shortly after, the boys are walking back to the garage with the wheels.

Con "Did your sister get upset when you told her that you were taking her bike wheels?"

Josh "No, she didn't say anything."

Con "You didn't ask her, did you?"

Josh "Nope! Did you ask your father whether you could borrow his golf cart wheels?"

Con "Sort of."

Josh "What do you mean sort of?"

Con "Um, not really."

Josh "We'd better make sure that we put them back after we finish. They'll never know the difference."

The garage is soon filled with the sound of hammers banging.

Con "I can't wait for the day my dad lets me use all his electric tools."

Josh "Well, I hope that's a long time from now. You're pretty scary with a plain old hammer!"

Con "Dad figures that by the time
he lets me use his tools I'll be so
old that I won't be able to lift
them."

Soon the boys have nailed more
wood to the plank to make a seat.
They have also managed to attach
axles and wheels to the plank.

Con "All we need to do now is tie some rope to the front axle so we can steer, and our race kart is ready to roll."

Josh (grinning) "You mean our *Formula 1 race car*!"

CHAPTER 4

Red Racing Machine

The boys catch sight of some paint cans on the shelves in the garage.

Con "I think we should borrow some of Dad's red paint. The kart will go a lot faster if it's painted red."

Josh "Yeah, red's a cool racing color!"

The boys take down the paint and paint the go-kart. They manage to get as much paint on the garage floor as they do on the go-kart.

Josh "It looks so cool."
Con "Yeah, totally hot. Now it's ready to rumble!"

Josh "So where are we gonna
race it?"

Con "What about Killer Hill?"

Josh "Okay—but first we're gonna
have to get a ton of safety gear.
That hill has messed up a
lot of skateboarders and bike
riders before."

Con and Josh leave the garage,
and moments later return wearing
safety gear.

Con "You've got so much on, you
look like an astronaut!"
Josh "Well, you totally need it when
you're a professional car racer,
you know."

Both boys have their bike helmets on. Con has pillows taped to his legs and his father's leather jacket on.

Josh "Your dad's old biker jacket looks really cool."

Con "Thanks, but I'm not so sure about those on you."

Josh "They're Mom's cleaning gloves. They're much better than any racing gloves I've ever seen."

Con "Well, let's go then! Killer Hill, here we come!"

CHAPTER 5

Killer Hill

Con and Josh tow their go-kart to Killer Hill—a grassy hill located in a park at the end of their street.

Con "Gee, it looks a lot steeper from up here than it does from the bottom of the hill."

Josh "Yeah, good thing we've got all this safety gear on."

Con "But I just remembered something we forgot."

Josh "What?"

Con "Brakes!"

Josh "It doesn't matter. It'll roll to a stop by itself when we get to the bottom."

Con "I hope so."

Josh "You scared? 'Cause *real* race car drivers love fear, you know!"

Con "Yeah, you're right. And we're the best race car drivers around— well, in this park, anyway. Let's do it!"

Con and Josh point the go-kart toward the bottom of the hill.

Con "Okay, this is it."
Josh "Who's gonna sit in front?"

The boys look at each other.

Con and Josh "You!!!"
Con "I think you should. You're the oldest."

Josh "Yeah, but only by two weeks. Okay, fine, I'll do it. Ready? GO!!!"

The boys hold on to the sides of the go-kart, take a running start, and then quickly jump in. Within seconds the cart is zooming down the hill.

Con and Josh

"AAAARRRGHHHH!!!!!!!!!!!"

Josh (shouting) "It's really hard to steer!"

Con (shouting) "We're gonna die!"

Con and Josh

"AAAARRRGHHHH!!!!!!!!!!!"

Suddenly the boys realize that they are heading directly for Con's dog, who has wandered in front of them.

Josh (shouting) "Oh no! We're heading straight for him!"

Con (shouting) "Look out! Josh! Josh! Turn! Turn!"

Josh (shouting) "I'm trying!"

Con (shouting) "He doesn't seen us. We're going to run over him."

Con and Josh

"AAAARRRGHHHH!!!!!!!!!!!!"

Just in time Josh steers the kart past the dog and on down the hill.

Con "That was close."
Josh "Lucky I'm a good dri—"
Con (shouting) "Look out for the—"

Smash! Josh and Con crash into a tree.

Josh "You okay?"

Con "Yeah. You?"

Josh "Yeah. That was unreal, we were flying. Now I know what race car drivers mean when they say they have 'the need for speed.'"

Josh "Yeah! We have the need for speed."

Con "Yeah! Let's do it again."

The boys hop out of the go-kart
and drag it back to the top of Killer
Hill. Seconds later, they're speeding
down it once again, this time with
Con in the front, steering.

Con "AAAARRRGHHHH!!!!!!!!!!!! It's
even worse up front than I thought."
Josh "Don't freak out. Just steer it
straight. Look out for that bump!"

But it's too late, and Josh, Con, and the go-kart fly into the air and then land with an almighty thud—the two front wheels snapping off completely.

Con "I don't think I have the need for speed anymore."
Josh "Yeah, I was thinking the same thing."

Con "But I do have the need
for food."

Josh "You must be a mind reader.
That's what I was thinking, too."

The boys pick themselves up,
collect the two front wheels, and
head home. They decide they've had
enough race car dreaming—at least
for today.

Racing Lingo

Josh

Con

brakes They lock up the wheels of a car to help it to stop.

burnout When the tires spin on the road and smoke comes from them.

drag The resistance that happens when a car or go-kart moves through the air.

scuffs Tires that have a couple of laps wear on them. "Stickers" are unused tires.

spinout When you lose control of the car that you are driving and go spinning around.

BOYZ RULE!

Racing Musts

☞ Always make sure that you wear a helmet.

☞ Wear really cool looking sunglasses.

☞ Watch NASCAR on TV to get racing tips.

☞ Paint your go-kart red. Red is a really fast color.

☞ Wear driving gloves. They may not help you go faster, but they help you look really cool!

☞ Check the steering before you take off. While you're at it, check your wheels too—make sure they're attached securely.

☞ Make sure that you have plenty of pillows to sit on.

☞ Try to go as fast as you can.

☞ Paint the number "1" on your go-kart.

☞ Avoid driving into trees. It's not good for your go-kart—or you.

☞ Take a few practice runs down some small hills before tackling the bigger ones.

BOYZ RULE!

Racing Instant Info

A black and white checkered flag is waved to the drivers at the end of a race.

If you happen to get the checkered flag waved at you, that means you have won the race!

A Formula 1 racing car can travel at a speed of 230 miles per hour (360 kilometers per hour).

Motorized go-kart racers can reach speeds of up to 90 miles per hour (144.8 kilometers per hour).

The first go-kart races took place in California, in 1956.

Most go-karts are about 5 feet (1.5 meters) in length.

Most go-karts have open sides, with railings for bumpers.

To build your own billycart you'll need at least 10 feet (3 meters) of lumber—and 4 wheels of course!

Think Tank

1 Where do Con and Josh get the wheels for their go-kart?

2 What is the name of the hill Con and Josh ride their go-kart on?

3 What do Con and Josh forget to put on their go-kart?

4 What is a burnout?

5 What does a checkered flag at the finish line mean?

6 Do you think you should wear a helmet when you drive a go-kart?

7 Josh and Con do not ask permission to take the materials they need to build their go-kart. What do you think about this? What do you think will happen?

8 Would you want to build a go-kart? If so, what would it look like?

Answers

8 Answers will vary.

7 Answers will vary.

6 You should always wear a helmet when driving a go-kart to protect your head in case you crash or tip over.

5 The checkered flag is waved at the finish line when the winner crosses it.

4 A burnout is when you make the wheels spin really fast in one spot.

3 They forget to put brakes on their go-kart.

2 The name of the hill is Killer Hill.

1 The wheels come from Josh's sister's bike and Con's dad's golf cart.

How did you score?

- If you got most of the answers correct, you're ready for your first go-kart race.

- If you got more than half of the answers correct, then you're ready for a go-kart race, but only as a codriver.

- If you got less than half of the answers correct, then you need to watch a few go-kart races first before you try it.

Felice →

← Phil

Hi Guys!

We have lots of fun reading and want you to, too. We both believe that being a good reader is really important and so cool.

Try out our suggestions to help you have fun as you read.

At school, why don't you use "Race Car Dreamers" as a play and you and your friends can be the actors. Set the scene for your play. Bring your bike helmet and safety gear to school to use as props, and use your acting skills and imagination to pretend that you are taking part in an important Formula 1 racing car event.

So...have you decided who is going to be Con and who is going to be Josh? Now, with your friends, read and act out our story in front of the class.

We have a lot of fun when we go to schools and read our stories. After we finish, the kids all clap really loudly. When you've finished your play your classmates will do the same. Just remember to look out the window—there might be a talent scout from a television station watching you!

Reading at home is really important and a lot of fun as well.

Take our books home and get someone in your family to read them with you. Maybe they can take on a part in the story.

Remember, reading is a whole lot of fun.

So, as the frog in the local pond would say, Read-it!

And remember, Boyz Rule!

BOYZ RULE!
When We Were Kids

Felice

Phil

Phil "Did you ever think you could've been a good race car driver?"

Felice "I used to think I could be the best! What about you?"

Phil "I know I would have been great. I learned to drive when I was really young."

Felice "How come?"

Phil "I lived on a farm and my father taught me to drive a tractor when I was only eight."

Felice "Did you have any accidents?"

Phil "One day I ran over a fence post."

Felice "Maybe you should've considered being a Demolition Derby driver instead."

BOYZ RULE!
What a Laugh!

Q What happens when a frog's car breaks down?

A It gets *toad* away.